TEENAGE MUTANT NINJA TURTLES™

LOOK OUT! IT'S TURTLE TITAN!

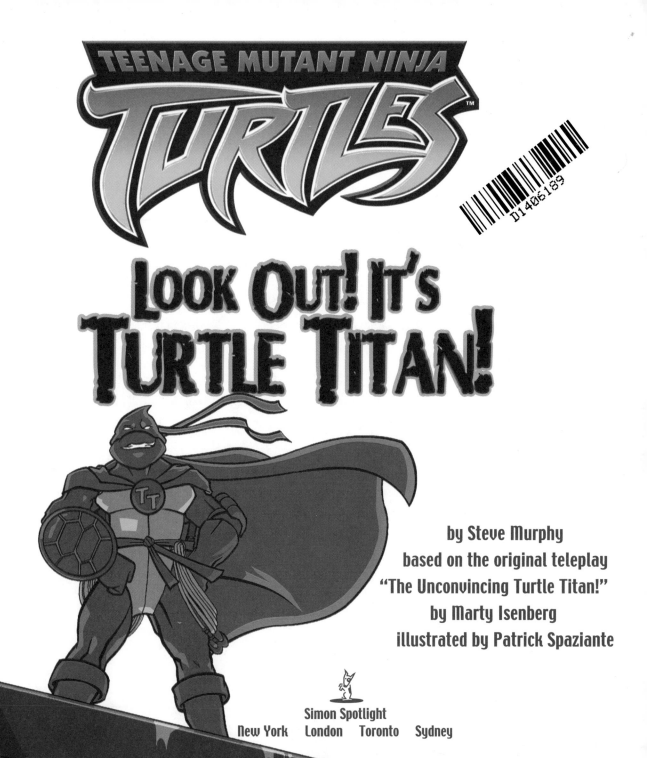

by Steve Murphy
based on the original teleplay
"The Unconvincing Turtle Titan!"
by Marty Isenberg
illustrated by Patrick Spaziante

Simon Spotlight
New York London Toronto Sydney

SIMON SPOTLIGHT

An imprint of Simon & Schuster Children's Publishing Division

1230 Avenue of the Americas, New York, New York 10020

Manufactured in the United States of America

First Edition   10 9 8 7 6 5 4 3 2 1

ISBN 0-689-86900-2

"We're supposed to be practicing the ninja art of invisibility, Mikey," whispered a voice from the shadows.

"I know, Leonardo," replied Michelangelo, not bothering to whisper. "But I'm tired of sneaking around all the time. I wish we could fight crime out in the open."

Across the street from the Turtles a building had caught fire.
"Hey, look!" exclaimed Donatello.
"We have to help that kid!" cried Michelangelo.

"Don't worry, Mikey," replied Leonardo. "The fire department has it covered. Besides, we'd get spotted."

"But what if they can't get her in time?" asked Michelangelo.

"Then *he* will," replied Raphael, pointing up toward the sky.

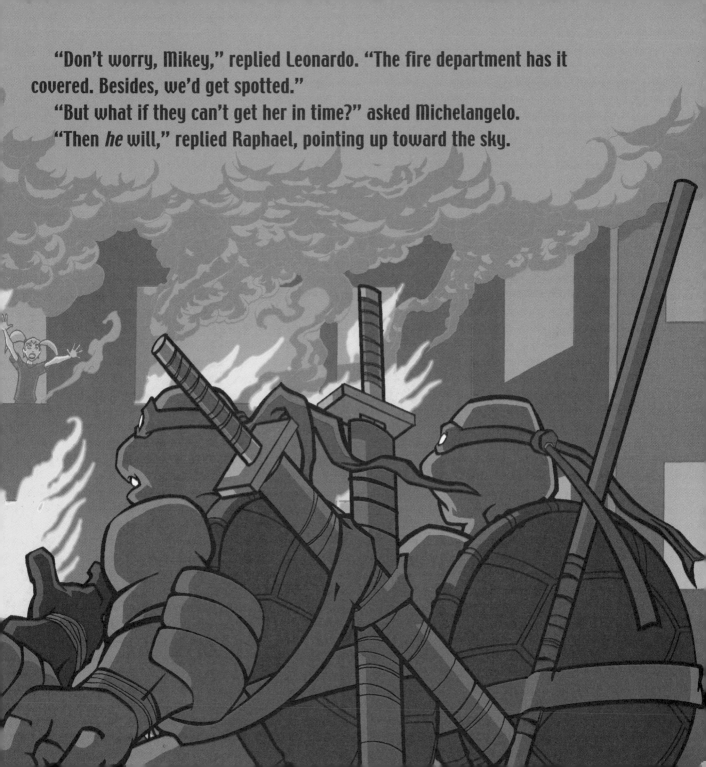

"Wow . . . it's really him. The Silver Sentry!" Michelangelo shouted.

The Turtles watched as the Silver Sentry flew straight into the building fire, swooped up the child, and set her down on the sidewalk.

"See, now there's a guy who doesn't have to stick to the shadows," said Michelangelo. "Look how much he's able to do."

"That's it, dudes! We should become superheroes!" exclaimed Michelangelo, impressed by the Silver Sentry's actions.

Donatello couldn't believe what his brother was saying. "I think you've got your bandanna on too tight, Mikey. The oxygen's not making it to your brain."

Back home at their sewer lair Michelangelo brought up his superhero idea again. "Superheroes never have to hold back because they're afraid someone might see them. And wouldn't it be nice to get a little credit for the good we do?" he asked.

Master Splinter spoke. "Your intentions are noble, Michelangelo. But you must never forget who you are. You are a ninja. Ninjas operate in the shadows."

"But couldn't we accomplish so much more out in the open?" asked Michelangelo. "There are many paths, my son," replied Splinter. "You must choose the one that is true to yourself."

Later that night Michelangelo went out on his own to fight crime. He had made a superhero costume out of old clothes and junk borrowed from his friend April O'Neil's antique store.

"Intro-ducing . . . Turtle Titan!" announced Michelangelo as he struck a heroic pose.

Michelangelo noticed that there was a robbery taking place at Crazy Manny's Electronic Store.

"Cowabunga!" cried Turtle Titan, as he swung toward the scene of the robbery in progress.

"Crazy Manny, why are you robbing your own store?" asked Turtle Titan. The man stared blankly and said nothing.

"Hey, what's that on your neck?" the superhero asked Crazy Manny, brushing a strange-looking insect from the storeowner's neck.

"Why are you robbing my store?!" exclaimed Crazy Manny, confused and frightened.

"Wait, *I'm* not breaking into your store. *You* were!" replied Turtle Titan. The hero then turned his gaze toward the strange insect scuttling away.

"Get out!" shouted Crazy Manny. "Police!"

And with that, Turtle Titan ran out of the store before the police showed up.

Later that night Turtle Titan tried to stop an out-of-control bus.

"Gee, this is crazy," the superhero said to himself, as he climbed inside the moving bus. "What's up with people tonight, anyway?"

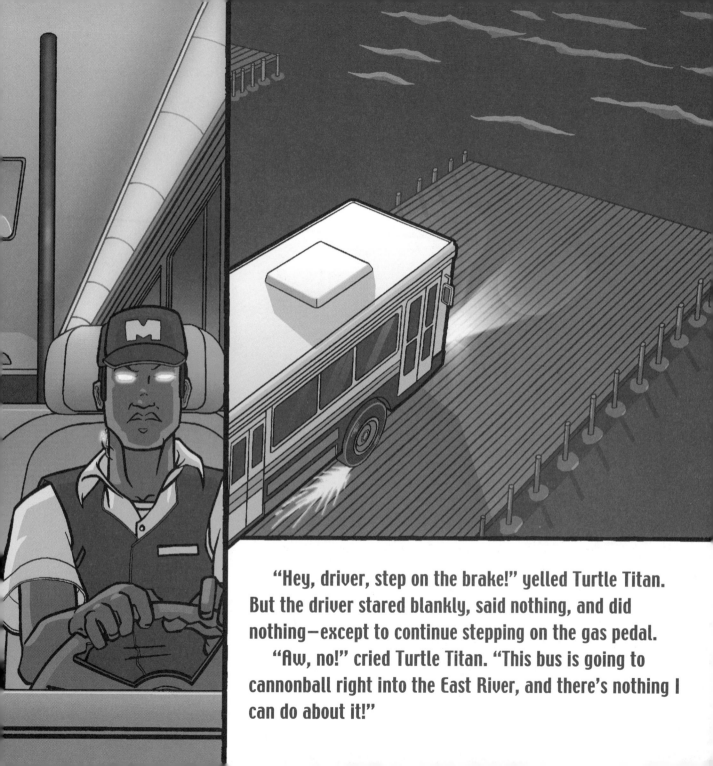

"Hey, driver, step on the brake!" yelled Turtle Titan. But the driver stared blankly, said nothing, and did nothing—except to continue stepping on the gas pedal.

"Aw, no!" cried Turtle Titan. "This bus is going to cannonball right into the East River, and there's nothing I can do about it!"

Suddenly, Silver Sentry appeared and carried the bus to safety.

"Silver Sentry! You saved our butts!" exclaimed Turtle Titan gratefully.

"No problem, citizen," replied the superhero.

Turtle Titan had removed the strange robotic insect from the bus driver's neck and handed it to Silver Sentry. "Someone's been controlling people with these things."

Silver Sentry examined the robo-bug. "This looks like the work of my arch-nemesis, Doctor Malignus. I think it's time I paid him a visit."

"Count me in!" cried Turtle Titan.

"I appreciate your help, kid, but you're in way over your head," said Silver Sentry. "Keep yourself out of sight while I deal with Malignus."

Turtle Titan watched as the Silver Sentry flew off to a warehouse used by his archenemy.

"You don't understand!" shouted Turtle Titan. "I became a superhero so that I *wouldn't* have to hide in the shadows anymore!"

"Ah, what does *he* know?" And with that said, the Turtle Titan ran across the Brooklyn Bridge and soon arrived at the villain's warehouse nearly out of breath.

"Gee, you'd think the arch-villain of a major superhero could afford a better place," Turtle Titan whispered to himself, as he studied his surroundings.

"Doctor Malignus, I presume?" asked Turtle Titan bravely. "Uh-oh . . . what have you done to Silver Sentry?"

"Nothing much. I've simply put him completely under my control. He's now my superpuppet," said the villain. "He'll do anything I say. And I say . . . destroy that turtle!"

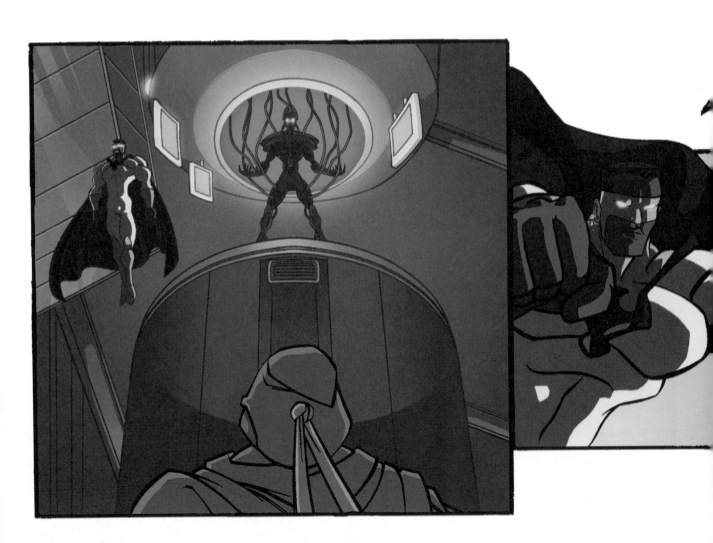

"Ooof!" exhaled Turtle Titan, the breath momentarily knocked out of him. "There's only one thing to do—I've got to be ninja-fast and try to nab that nasty robo-bug!"

"Nice move, Turtle Titan," said a thankful Silver Sentry, now free from the arch-villain's mind control.

"It's over, Malignus. You've lost," said the superhero, as he turned to face his enemy.

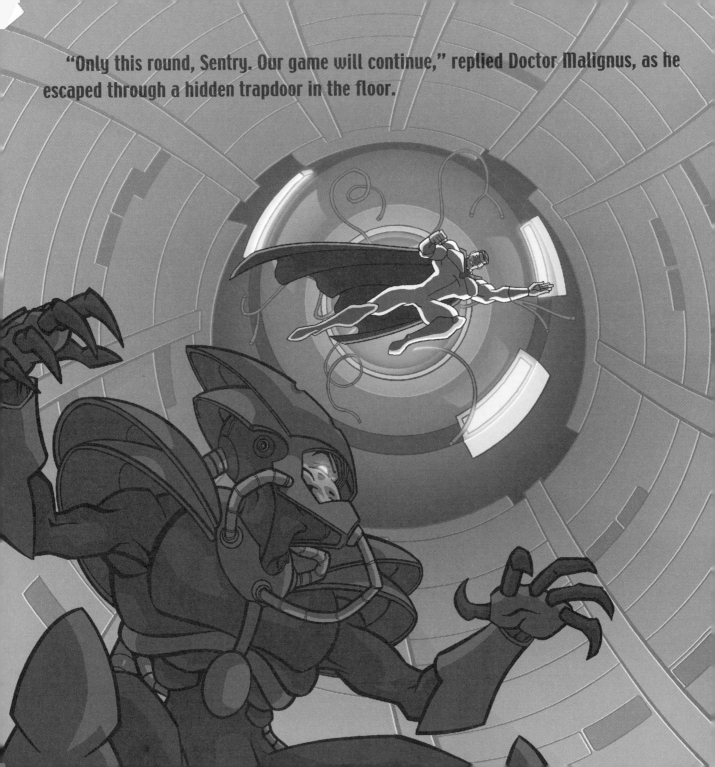

"Only this round, Sentry. Our game will continue," replied Doctor Malignus, as he escaped through a hidden trapdoor in the floor.

Who needs a shield and grapple? thought Michelangelo, as he emerged from the shadows no longer wearing his Turtle Titan costume.

"Game over, Malignus!" said Michelangelo. It was the last thing the villain heard before the Ninja Turtle's flying dropkick stopped him cold.

Afterward Michelangelo thought about his night's adventure.
"I guess I can do a lot more good for this town working from the shadows—the only way a Ninja Turtle can," he said to himself. "*That* is my true path."